WRITERS REPUBLIC

Endless Dreams

Shakeyia Jackson

WRITERS REPUBLIC L.L.C.
515 Summit Ave. Unit R1
Union City, NJ 07087, USA

Website: *www.writersrepublic.com*
Hotline: *1-877-656-6838*
Email: *info@writersrepublic.com*

Ordering Information:
Quantity sales. Special discounts are available on quantity purchases by corporations, associations, and others. For details, contact the publisher at the address above.

Library of Congress Control Number: 2020914579
ISBN-13:   978-1-64620-538-7   [Paperback Edition]
                        978-1-64620-539-4   [Digital Edition]

Rev. date: 08/03/2020

To my firstborn and only son, your curiosity about the world is amazing always follow your dreams.

To my beautiful baby girl remember the sky is the limit!

Thanks to my husband and family for always believing in me and to my high school teacher Mrs. McCready for always being a message or phone call away and giving out great advice.

I'm A'donnis, and I'm five years old. My mom loves to tell me about different careers I can take up when I grow up. On Monday, she said that I could be a Lawyer. I asked her to tell me what lawyers do, and she said, "A'donnis, lawyers give advice and help people in court."

"How do lawyers help people?"

"Lawyers help people by defending them in court," my mom said, kissing me on my right cheek.

So that day, I pretended to be a lawyer. I took the biggest case ever and defended an innocent person.

"Your honor, my client is innocent!" I screamed while pointing my finger towards Spiderman.

On Tuesday, my mom told me that I could be a Doctor because Doctors help people stay healthy and make them feel better when they are sick.

"Whoa! I would love to be a Doctor," I said and ran happily to my bedroom.

Thinking like a Doctor, I put on my long white shirt, trying to dress like our family Doctor.

I picked up my Iron man action guy from the table and pretended to check his heart rate and bones.

7

Later that day, I asked my little sister, Justice, if she could be my patient, and she agreed.

So, I put on my clown costume nose and colorful hair because I know how children can get scared, and I wanted to make it fun.

On Wednesday, my mom told me about an astronaut and said I could be one if I wanted. She said astronauts study space and love heights. In my room, I imagined myself flying to the moon and looking to see if there are other planets where humans can survive. I felt happy.

11

On Thursday, my mom said I could be a zoologist or a paleontologist.

"Uh, oh! These are some big words," I said playfully.

My mom explained that zoologists work with animals while paleontologists study fossils they find and try to discover how old they are.

"Honey, I mentioned these careers because I know how much you love animals and dinosaurs' fossils."

She's right. Just look at my room, I have more animals and dinosaurs than any other toy.

That day, I used my paintbrush and pretended to be in a desert uncovering fossils and studying my favorite ocean animal, Octopus.

13

On Friday, my mom smiled at me and said, "A'donnis, there are so many jobs and careers in the world. But do you know what I want for you?"

I shook my head, and she continued, "Baby, I want you to be happy and follow your dreams," she said and gave me a tight hug.

I know she wants the best for me, but what will I be?

15

Glossary

Career: The job you do or choose for a certain period.

Lawyer : A lawyer is a professional who is trained to give and help people in situations that involve legal matters.

Astronaut : A person who is trained to travel in a space craft.

Doctor: A male or female that practices medicine that heals the sick and keeps others healthy. They also predict how long it will take for us to get healthy.

Zoologist: Scientists who study animal life and their habitats. They predict how long animals can live and how they survive.

Paleontologist: Scientists who study plants and animals that lived millions of years ago. They use fossils to determine how long an animal lived and how big it was.

CPSIA information can be obtained
at www.ICGtesting.com
Printed in the USA
LVHW070318260920
667178LV00030B/2399